D1187607

The First Snow

Donnaleen Rasmussen

Copyright © 2020 Donnaleen Rasmussen
All rights reserved
First Edition

PAGE PUBLISHING, INC.
Conneaut Lake, PA

First originally published by Page Publishing 2020

ISBN 978-1-6624-1704-7 (hc)
ISBN 978-1-6624-1703-0 (digital)

Printed in the United States of America

The First Snow

Dedicated to Joy Mills

T'was the morning of
the very first snow.
We peered through the window
our faces aglow.

For snowflakes were dancing
and prancing around,
As they swirled and floated
their way to the ground.

We donned our coats
our mittens and hats.
We flew out the door
with Kitty and Kats–

We huffed and we puffed
as we rolled balls of snow,
little ones, big ones
all piled in a row.

3

We ran to the house
for our box of "stuff"
of caps and gingerbread
of scarves and a muff.

We dragged it through
the snow so deep
and left it there
in a great snow heap.

Then we heard Mother's voice
calling through the flakes,
"Come in for supper
cocoa and cakes."

We headed for home
and turned to say,
"We'll be out tomorrow
to play all day."

The sun went down.
The stars come out.
All was quiet—
then came a shout!

6

Get up, snowy friends!
Let's have a party.
Get up get ready,
let's not be tardy.

They scurried there
and hurried here.
"What shall we wear
Oh dear, oh dear."

They all gathered 'round
the box sitting there
and all of sudden
things flew in the air!

8

Canes of candy,
hats and holly,
coats and carrots
and gingerbread
jolly.

Mittens and muffs
and shiny black boots,
socks and scarves
and a horn that
toots!

TOOT
TOOT

They hurriedly dressed
in the clothes so fine
then gathered round
the table to dine.

11

They sipped hot cocoa
with canes of red
and stuffed their tummies
with gingerbread.

Then they danced around
and laughed and sang,
'round and 'round and 'round
while silver bells rang.

They went so fast
they could hardly stop...
and when they did
they landed—*kerplop!*

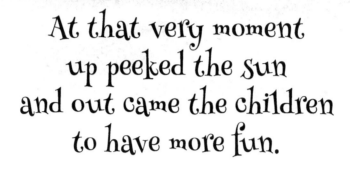

At that very moment
up peeked the sun
and out came the children
to have more fun.

O'er the hills they trudged
through the snow
looking for the snowballs
they left in a row.

They stood still in their tracks
as before their eyes,
the snowy friends jumped
and yelled...

"Come play with us," they said,
"We'll dance and sing,
come play with us
until it's spring."

"We'll drink hot cocoa
with canes of red
and fill our tummies
with gingerbread."

So they all danced 'round
and laughed and sang,
round and round
while silver bells rang.

19

They drank hot cocoa
with canes of red
and stuffed their tummies
with gingerbread.

20

They all became
such splendid friends

and that is how
this story ends.

About the Author

Doni studied art in college and had the opportunity to work as an artist at Hallmark Cards in Kansas City, Missouri, for several years. She is an avid gardener and volunteers at Word of Life camps in the Adirondacks of New York during the summer taking care of their flower gardens.

As a mother of three, she had the opportunity to read many bedtime stories to her children. Her sons especially loved *The Cat in the Hat* and *Mr. Toad*. The imagination is a wonderful, happy place to go, and hopefully all children can experience the joy of reading and being read to.

CPSIA information can be obtained
at www.ICGtesting.com
Printed in the USA
BVHW020251190721
612207BV00001B/3